ANIMAL BABIES
LIKE TO PLAY

BALZER + BRAY
An Imprint of HarperCollins Publishers

Words by JENNIFER ADAMS   Pictures by MARY LUNDQUIST

For Bill
–J. A.

For Dylan
–M. L.

Balzer + Bray is an imprint of HarperCollins Publishers.

Animal Babies Like to Play
Text copyright © 2019 by Jennifer Adams
Illustrations copyright © 2019 by Mary Lundquist
All rights reserved. Manufactured in China.

ISBN 978-0-06-239447-7

The artist used pencil, watercolor, and gouache on watercolor paper to create the art for this book.
Typography by Aurora Parlagreco
18 19 20 21 22 SCP 10 9 8 7 6 5 4 3 2 1
❖
First Edition

Alligator baby wants to play.

Bunny baby says, "Okay."

Cat baby reads a book.

Dog baby sleeps in a nook.

Elephant baby draws with chalk.

F ox baby goes on a walk.

Giraffe baby likes skipping rocks.

Hippo baby likes
building with blocks.

Iguana baby wants to run away.

Jaguar baby says,
"Oh, please stay."

Koala baby plays hide-and-seek.

Lamb baby says, "Don't you peek!"

Monkey baby makes a wish.

Narwhal baby catches fish.

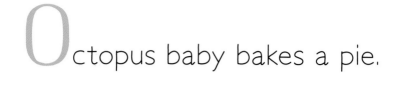

Octopus baby bakes a pie.

Peacock baby lets out a sigh.

Quail baby looks at the moon.

Reindeer baby lost his balloon.

Squirrel baby eats a snack.

Turtle baby plays with jacks.

Ulysses butterfly baby runs with a net.

Vulture baby says,
"You haven't caught one yet!"

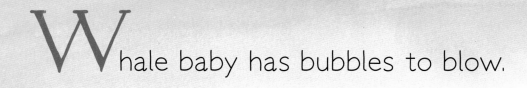

Whale baby has bubbles to blow.

X-ray tetra baby collects things that glow.

Yak baby says,
"I can't find my friend."

Zebra baby comes
out in the end!